Our Community Garden

Published by
Beyond Words Publishing, Inc.
20827 NW Cornell Road, Suite 500
Hillsboro, Oregon 97124
503-531-8700

Editor: Barbara Leese
Cover Design: Jerry Soga

Printed in Korea

ISBN: 1-58270-109-1

Library of Congress Control Number: 2003027398

The corporate mission of Beyond Words Publishing, Inc:
Inspire to Integrity

Library of Congress Cataloging-in-Publication Data

Pollak, Barbara.
   Our community garden / written and illustrated by Barbara Pollak.-- 1st ed.
      p. cm.
   Summary: A diverse group of people in San Francisco shares the work and
fun of a community garden.
   ISBN 1-58270-109-1 (hardcover)
   [1. Community gardens--Fiction. 2. Gardening--Fiction. 3. Community
life--Fiction. 4. San Francisco (Calif.)--Fiction.] I. Title.

PZ7.P7575Ou 2004
   [E]--dc22   2003027398

Our Community Garden

Written and Illustrated
by Barbara Pollak

BEYOND
WORDS
Publishing
I N C

I'm Audrey Aubergine.

My friends and I live in San Francisco next to a community garden on a steep hill.

Every day after school and during the summer we play and work in the garden.

Sometimes we play
hide-and-seek in the giant
sunflowers that grow along
the fence.

Sometimes we spend all
afternoon counting ladybugs and honeybees.

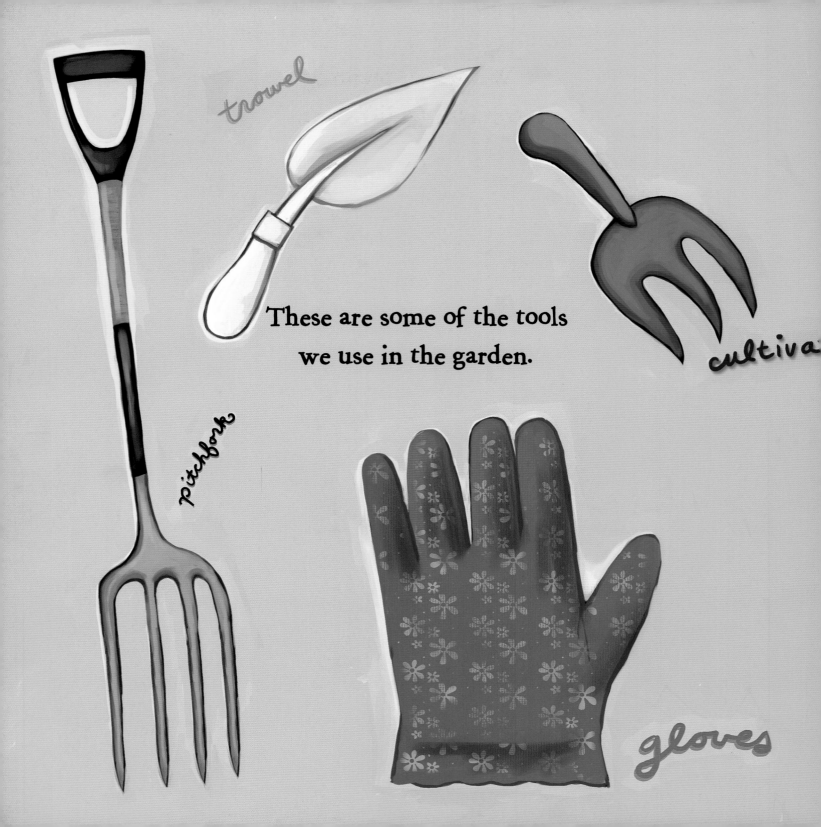

trowel

cultiva[tor]

pitchfork

These are some of the tools
we use in the garden.

gloves

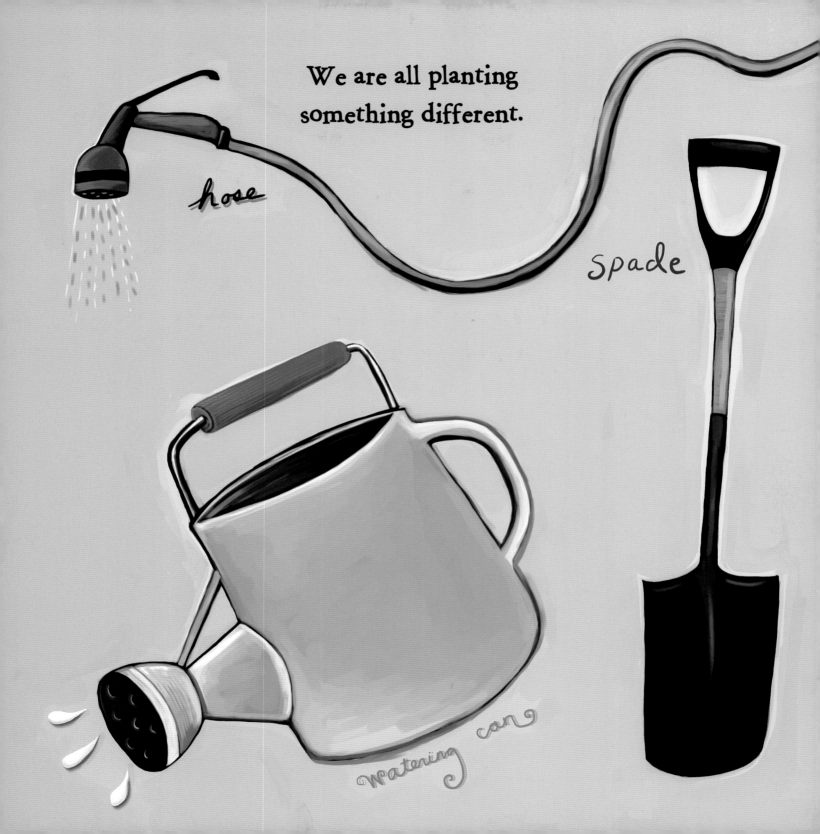

Tomás is growing tomatillos and hot peppers for his world-famous salsa. He says it's going to be hotter than ever this year.

Tomatillos look like little green paper lanterns.

My best friend Cassandra is growing short orange carrots with red cores. Most of the growing happens under the ground.

She keeps a garden diary
so she knows when
they'll be ready.

lettuce

carrots

March 10- Planted seeds
in 5 rows

TOMATOES

april-planted red+yellow
cherry tomatoes,
beefsteak, and black
krim varieties
Mid-may- transplanted
seedlings into ground

snap bean

March- built small trellis
april-started seedlings

Alison Chin, our next door neighbor, is
growing a special type of long, thin green
bean called "asparagus" bean.

"They're great in my mom's tofu and bean
stir-fry," she says.

This year I'm growing eggplants.
Eggplants come in many varieties,
but I'm going to try growing the
long, skinny purple ones.

Every day when I get home
and change out of my school
clothes I go to the garden
and look at my eggplants
to see if there has been
any progress.

I keep the soil moist and pick out the weeds.

centipede

Sometimes I dig for worms and
watch them wiggle and squirm.

rove beetle

earthworm

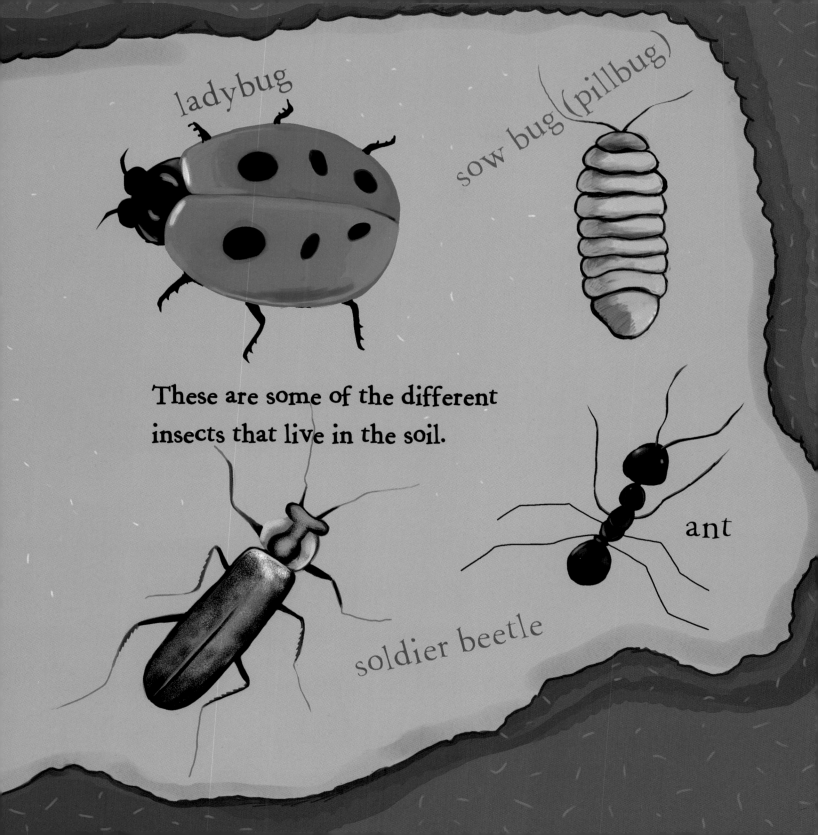

ladybug

sow bug (pillbug)

These are some of the different insects that live in the soil.

soldier beetle

ant

One day my friends and I were playing hide-and-seek when Cassandra noticed a small green shoot sticking up from the ground.

"My carrots are coming up!"
she shouted happily.

Tomás and I made up a special dance to celebrate.

Soon, Tomás' tomatillos started
to grow, followed by Alison's
asparagus beans and my
skinny purple eggplants.

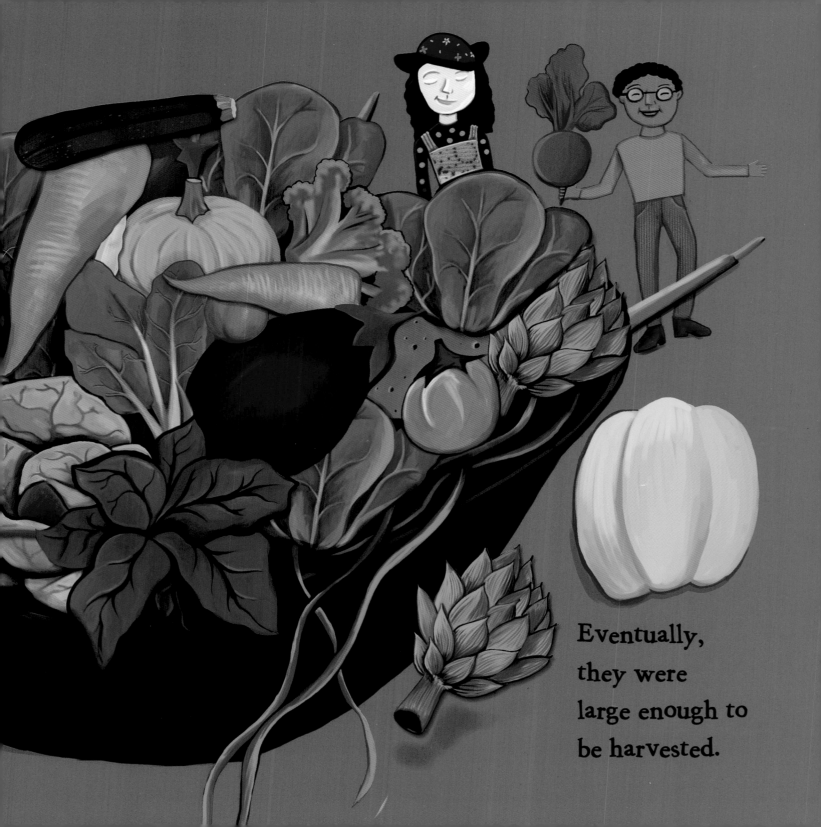

Eventually,
they were
large enough to
be harvested.

Today we have harvested enough vegetables to have a giant feast. Everyone in the neighborhood is invited to bring a special dish made from vegetables they grew in the community garden. We're having salsa, stir-fry, eggplant stew, potato pie, and carrot cake. Yum! I can't wait.

.Potato.Pie.

Salsa:

tomatillos   fresh cilantro

plum tomatoes   1 onion, chopped

cumin   1 small lime

1 hot pepper , diced

3 cloves garlic

For more information on how you can
start your own garden visit:

www.happypix.com/audrey.html